D0572638

J   Aiello, Barbara.

          Friends for life.

$12.95

DATE		
MAY 1 0 1991	JAN 2 1998	
JUN 1 3 1991	FEB 0 5 2000	
JUL 1 7 1991	MAR 1 8 2000	
AUG 1 4 1991	JUN 1 0 2000	
SEP 2 0 1991	SEP 2 7 2000	
MAR 7 1992	OCT 2 4 2000	
MAY 2 1 1992	NOV 2 1 2000	
SEP 1 8 1996	FEB 2 7 2001	
	SEP 2 1 2001	

© THE BAKER & TAYLOR CO.

Friends For Life

THE KIDS ON THE BLOCK BOOK SERIES

Friends For Life

Featuring Amy Wilson

Barbara Aiello and Jeffrey Shulman
Illustrated by Loel Barr

TWENTY-FIRST CENTURY BOOKS
FREDERICK, MARYLAND

Twenty-First Century Books
38 South Market Street
Frederick, Maryland 21701

Printed in the United States of
America

9 8 7 6 5 4 3

Special Sales:

The Kids on the Block Book
Series is available at quantity dis-
counts with bulk purchase for
educational, charitable, business,
or sales promotional use. For information, please write to:
Marketing Director, Twenty-First
Century Books, 38 South Market
Street, Frederick, Maryland,
21701.

Library of Congress Cataloging-in-Publication Data

Aiello, Barbara.
    Friends for life: featuring Amy Wilson / by Barbara
Aiello and Jeffrey Shulman; illustrated by Loel Barr.
    (The Kids on the Block book series)
    Summary: When the members of the fifth-grade video club find out
their club sponsor has AIDS, they have a variety of reactions before
learning more about the disease and deciding to stick by her.
    ISBN 0-941477-03-7
    [1. AIDS (Disease)—Fiction. I. Shulman, Jeffrey, 1951– .
II. Barr, Loel, ill. III. Title. IV. Series: Aiello, Barbara. Kids on the
Block book series.
PZ7.A26924Fr   1988   88-29251
[Fic]—dc19

To the children who teach us about differences—
and similarities

CHAPTER 1

"C'mon, everybody," Natalie was saying above the noise of the Video Club meeting. "*Somebody* must have an idea for a title."

"Hey, how about *Swamp Monsters*?" asked Robbie. Robbie Jenkins: you could always count on him to come up with something gruesome. He had a vivid imagination, at least for blood and guts and swamp things and stuff like that.

"Yeah," Jason said. "That's more like it. How about *Return of the Dead Swamp Monsters*? That will pack the theater, won't it?" Jason was okay, but why did he always have to go along with Robbie?

"It may just *unpack* the theater," Natalie said firmly. I liked Natalie a lot. She was a teacher's aide at Woodburn, back when I was in the second grade. I was pretty shy then—well, I guess I'm pretty shy now, too—but Natalie always took the time to see how I was doing. She made me feel . . . somehow . . . important.

"We're trying to get people to come see the movie," Leslie said, "not turn them away." That was Leslie, all right. I admired the way she always spoke her mind. There was nothing shy about her.

"Or make them sick," I said softly. And that was me—Amy Wilson. It was barely a whisper, but everybody turned to look at me. I guess they were surprised to hear from "Quiet Little Amy." "What about *The Purple Slime from Seldon Swamp*?" I suggested.

The Woodburn School Video Club was about to make its first real movie. It was only about a month ago that Natalie—

Natalie Gregg, our club sponsor—told us about a special media contest for fifth and sixth graders. Only a month ago! It seemed like we met every day to talk about our plans.

"Well, what about *The Purple Slime from Seldon Swamp?*" I said again.

You see, the story was about how some kids decide to explore the old Seldon Swamp (they say it's haunted) on Halloween night. But it's not really haunted: it's being used by drug smugglers who pretend it's haunted to frighten everyone else away. And when we—I mean, when the kids find out the truth, they make their own monster out of purple slime and scare the smugglers out of the swamp and right into the hands of the police. The whole thing was Robbie Jenkins's idea. It figures, doesn't it?

"I like it," Leslie said. "I think I like it."

"Sounds good to me," said Brenda.

That's when Robbie and Jason started shouting "Swamp Monsters, Swamp Monsters" and making creepy faces. They thought they were hysterical, I guess.

"They give me the creeps," Leslie whispered to me. "All the time."

"Okay, that's enough," said Natalie. "Let's take a vote. All those in favor of *Return of the Dead Swamp Monsters* raise your hand." Two hands shot right up. Robbie and Jason were sticking together. "All those in favor of *The Purple Slime from Seldon Swamp* raise your hand." And would you believe it? Seven hands went up—and my title was the winner! You could tell that Robbie and Jason were disappointed. They wanted to start a special Woodburn Dead Swamp Monsters Club.

"I'm afraid," Natalie told them, "you'll have to find another sponsor for that one."

"Hey," Jason asked, "how are we going to make a purple slime monster, anyway?"

"I guess we could always get Leslie to play the starring role," Robbie laughed.

"Very funny, Robbie Jenkins," Leslie said back. "You're a regular comedian."

"Enough!" shouted Natalie. "That's a good question." It was a good question, but it didn't seem like anyone had a good answer.

I raised my hand sort of halfway.

"Is something cooking in that brain of yours, Amy?" Natalie asked.

Something was cooking, all right. "Well," I said, "I guess we could make spaghetti and jello and messy stuff like that and then put purple food coloring in it. We could smear it all over the person who plays the monster."

"That's gross and disgusting," said Robbie. "I like it!"

"Way to go, Amy," Jason said. "We may have to make you a member of the Dead Swamp Monsters Club."

"Thanks, but no thanks, Jason," I replied.

Natalie put her arm around my shoulder. "I think we've got it," she said. "I think we've got a winner." A cheer went up from the club members. Everyone was so excited.

"First prize, for sure!" shouted Brenda.

Even quiet Amy Wilson raised her voice: "Hollywood, here we come!" I hollered.

We were so happy we all marched home chanting "Purple Slime, Purple Slime!" The whole world must have thought we were crazy!

CHAPTER 2

There was nothing but purple slime on the brain of every member of the Video Club for the next few days. Robbie and Brenda wrote and rewrote the script, and Jason, Leslie, and I worked on the production details, like costumes and scenery. That's how we found ourselves in the art supply room.

"It's dark in here," Jason said. I think he was a little bit afraid.

"It usually is before you turn on the lights," Leslie told him.

I reached up and pulled the light switch on. We were in a big room filled with shelves of paint and paper. There were also all kinds of decorations and things.

"Look at this," I said, holding up a goblin mask with dripping eyeballs and a drooling mouth. Jason and Leslie jumped back. "Must be from last year's Halloween 'Ghost Festival.'"

"It's a good thing Robbie's not here," Leslie said. "He would go nuts."

"He *is* nuts," I thought. But I didn't say it.

We were so busy exploring the supply room that at first we didn't notice what sounded like an argument on the other side of the supply room wall.

"Shhhh," I said softly. "That sounds like Mr. Mohammadi's voice."

"Wow," Jason whispered, "somebody must be mad."

There was a fight, all right. "That's Mr. Mohammadi," I said, "and that sounds like Mr. and Mrs. Jenkins." We could hear it loud and clear. I quickly reached up to switch off the supply room light.

10

"Don't tell me you're just the assistant principal!" Mr. Jenkins was almost screaming. "You're in charge for now. And we want an answer—now!"

"That's a reasonable request, a very reasonable request. If we can just go over this"—

"I don't want to go over anything," Mrs. Jenkins interrupted. "I just want to know the truth. The truth about her."

Hunkered down in the dark room, we wondered what was going on. The truth about what? About whom?

"If she has AIDS, we want to know." It was Mrs. Jenkins again. "We have a right to know."

AIDS? We had heard about AIDS. Someone from somewhere talked about it at Woodburn several months ago, but nobody paid much attention to it. All I knew was that people who had it died. That was all I knew—and all I wanted to know. "What's going on?" I wondered out loud.

"Of course, we will keep you informed if your child is in any kind of danger," Mr. Mohammadi repeated. You could tell he was trying to be calm. "We will certainly look into it."

"*Look into it?* I want to know what you will *do about it.*" Mr. Jenkins said angrily.

"If she has AIDS," Mr. Mohammadi explained, "we will take the appropriate action"—

"Appropriate action?" Mrs. Jenkins interrupted. "The only appropriate action is to get her out of the school and away from our children. Get Natalie Gregg out of Woodburn!"

We heard the Jenkins storm out of Mr. Mohammadi's office, slamming the door. It seemed like the whole supply room shook, nearly toppling over a row of goblin heads. The room was dark and completely quiet. No one knew what to say.

"AIDS?" Jason said. "Mrs. Gregg has AIDS?"

"Just wait a minute, Jason," Leslie responded. "We don't know that for sure. I don't think we should start spreading rumors. Right, Amy? Amy?"

I was just sitting there in my own world. I barely heard Leslie. I barely heard myself say, "Right," but I didn't know what to think. I felt somehow lost. And I was glad we were in the dark.

"Mrs. Gregg has AIDS?" Jason repeated.

It was like the word "AIDS" itself had cast some sort of magical spell over us, in a moment changing our world and changing us. Everything seemed so strange. And my friends seemed like strangers.

"What's going to happen now?" I asked.

CHAPTER 3

I don't know how, but the news about Natalie spread through Woodburn faster than chicken pox. Everybody was talking about it, especially the Video Club.

"But we don't even know for sure that she has it." I was almost crying.

"Well, my parents don't care whether we know for sure or not," Robbie said. "I'm out of the Video Club."

"I guess *The Purple Slime from Seldon Swamp* just wasn't meant to be," Brenda added. "Who wants to be around someone with AIDS? Not me!"

"My parents haven't made *me* quit the club," said Jason.

"They will, believe me," Robbie argued.

"Maybe they will, and maybe they won't," I said. "Why don't we try to talk to them about it?"

"*Talk?* What is there to talk about?" Robbie asked.

"What do you really know about AIDS, anyway?" I asked.

"What I know," Robbie asserted, "is that when you get it, you're dead meat." He drew an imaginary knife across his throat. "Dead meat," he said again. "What I know is that anybody can get it. What I know is that I'm not getting anywhere near someone with AIDS. That's what I know!"

Robbie stomped right out of the meeting. So did Brenda, Matthew, and several others. Leslie stood up to go.

"You, too?" I asked.

"I'm sorry," she said, "but this isn't fun anymore. This is for real. Natalie's my friend, too, but this is life or death, Amy. I'm getting out before it's too late. I'm sorry. But I'm scared."

That left me and Jason. We looked glumly at each other. Jason tried to smile. It looked like the smile of a dead swamp monster. "So much for Hollywood," I sighed, trying to cast off this strange spell of fear we were under. But to tell the truth, I was scared, too.

"Yeah," said Jason.

That was all there was to say.

CHAPTER 4

I walked home from the meeting by myself. I just didn't feel like being with the other kids. Ever since I found out about Natalie, I don't know how to explain it, but I felt . . . lonely.

I stopped by Woodburn Park. It was on my way home, and I liked to sit by the lake and watch the ducks whenever I wasn't in a hurry. I certainly wasn't in a hurry today. I was walking at a snail's pace.

The lake is a beautiful blue when the sun is out. You could see the clouds floating on its smooth surface and the bright rocks on the muddy bottom. There was hardly a breeze in the still air: there was hardly a ripple to be seen.

I sat by the lake for a long time, trying to figure things out. What should I do now? Should I talk to Natalie? Should I tell my parents? What would they do? I couldn't understand why

Natalie didn't tell the club, why she didn't tell me. I thought we were friends.

I remembered times when I was at Natalie's house. They were good times. There was the Video Club picnic. Jason and Robbie were chasing everybody with water balloons, and when they held them up to throw them, they burst—right on their own heads. I could see Natalie and Leslie and Brenda holding their sides and laughing. Even Jason and Robbie thought it was pretty funny. I remembered the first meeting of the Video Club. It was Natalie who said we could make a movie: "I know you can do it," she said. "I believe in you."

Now look what had happened. Everything was ruined. Why did Natalie let this happen? Why did she get AIDS in the first place? AIDS. It seemed like everywhere I turned I heard the "AIDS" word. I could see the headline in the school newspaper: "Video Club Sponsor Gets AIDS." I could hear the anger in Mr. Jenkins's voice. It reminded me of a movie I watched with my Dad. I forget the name, but it's about a monster some scientist makes, and how everybody hates him, and how they chase him through the night with burning torches, and how they kill him. "If you're scared, honey," Dad said, "why don't we turn it off?" But I wasn't frightened of the monster. I was scared when I saw everybody chasing him. There was so much hatred in *them*.

And now it wasn't just a movie. It was really happening—and I didn't know what to think or do.

The lake was still clear as glass, but when I looked at it, it seemed dark and cloudy to me.

CHAPTER 5

I let myself in the front door. The house seemed big and awfully quiet. I wished my Mom were home.

When I get home from school, I usually find something to eat and turn on the television for a while. I'm not supposed to watch television in the afternoon, but I just turn it on for a little while, and I don't really pay much attention, anyway. It's just to have some company, really.

I plopped myself down on the couch. There was a talk show on, but I wasn't listening. I wasn't, that is, until I heard some man talking about AIDS. That got my attention, sure enough. He was a friendly looking guy. He reminded me of an old sea captain. He had on a uniform, but I couldn't tell whether he was a soldier or a doctor. He looked like both. I heard him say the "AIDS" word, and I began to listen more carefully. One thing he said grabbed my attention and wouldn't let go: "Today," he said, "every home in America has received a pamphlet about AIDS. You must read it. You must share it with your loved ones."

I wondered if he really meant what he said about every home in America getting a pamphlet on AIDS. Well, I figured, there was one way to find out. I stuck my head out the front door and glanced into the mailbox. Sure enough, there was a big, blue and white pamphlet along with the rest of the mail. I figured that was it. I looked around to see if anyone was watching. The coast was clear. I took the pamphlet and headed up to my room.

I knew it was wrong, but I opened it anyway. I don't know why I did it. I just felt this need to know what this was all about. *I just felt this need to know*. I read the first page.

Understanding AIDS
A Message From The Surgeon General

"This brochure has been sent to you by the Government of the United States. In preparing it, we have consulted with the top experts in the country.

I feel it is important that you have the best information now available for fighting the AIDS virus, a health problem that the President has called 'Public Enemy, Number One.'

Stopping AIDS is up to you, your family, and your loved ones.

Some of the issues involved in this brochure may not be things you are used to discussing openly. I can easily understand that. But now you must discuss them. We all must know about AIDS. Read this brochure and talk about it with those you love. Get involved. Many schools, synagogues, churches, and community groups offer AIDS education activities.

I encourage you to practice reponsible behavior based on understanding and strong personal values. This is what you can do to stop AIDS."

It was signed by a man named C. Everett Koop. It was the man on the television, the one who looked like a sea captain.

I didn't understand all of the message. But I did understand one part: "Get involved." I just couldn't quit the club. I just couldn't run out on Natalie. I had to know more.

I opened up the pamphlet carefully. I didn't know what to expect. There were all kinds of questions: How Do You Get AIDS? What Behavior Puts You At Risk? What Does Someone With AIDS Look Like? What About Dating? What Is All The Talk About Condoms? There was so much I didn't know. There was so much more I didn't understand.

There were pictures of doctors and counselors, and there were lots of pictures of ordinary people, too—just regular people talking about how they got AIDS and what it's like to have AIDS. I couldn't help but stare at them. One of the women looked so pretty, with big dark eyes that reminded me of Natalie's.

Just then I heard the front door open and knew my Mom was home. I hurriedly put the pamphlet away.

"Amy, are you up there?" she shouted up the steps.

"Yeah, Ma," I shouted back. "Doing my homework."

I had never lied to my mother before, at least not about anything important. Not about anything like this. "What's happening to me?" I asked myself. Sneaking around with my parent's mail. *Lying to my mother!* I couldn't explain it. It just seemed that every time the "AIDS" word came up, people changed. They changed into something mean and ugly. It was like AIDS made people turn into monsters. I just didn't want to see that happen to my parents.

"Please," I said, talking to the picture of Mr. Koop. I don't know why I was trying to talk to a picture: I guess I just needed to talk to someone. "Please, don't let that happen to them."

CHAPTER 6

It didn't.

That night, during dinner, the phone rang. There was nothing out of the ordinary about that, but it was the start of an extraordinary chain of events.

"Who was that, dear?" Mom asked Dad as he returned to the table.

"That was Mr. Mohammadi," he responded, looking at me. I gulped down the last of my milk.

"Mr. Mohammadi, the assistant principal?" Mom asked.

"The very same," Dad said. "It seems that there's quite a storm brewing over at Woodburn. Amy may be able to fill us in."

"Amy?" asked Mom.

"Well," Dad went on, "it appears that the center of the storm is the Woodburn Video Club. According to Mr. Mohammadi, the Video Club sponsor has AIDS."

"Not Natalie?" You could hear the concern in Mom's voice.

"But it isn't true!" I shouted. "It's just a rumor the kids are spreading."

"There's no need to shout, Amy," Dad said. "I don't think it is just a rumor. Natalie herself told Mr. Mohammadi about it. I guess there are some very angry parents."

"And some very angry students," I added.

"Including you?" Mom asked.

"No. Well, yes. I mean, I don't know." No one had really asked me what my feelings were before. I hadn't asked myself. "I mean, why didn't she tell us? Maybe if she had just told us, everyone wouldn't be so scared. They're scared to death. I mean it. Why didn't she just tell us what this AIDS thing is about?"

Dad spoke after a while. "Well, maybe she was scared, too."

"Scared? Scared of AIDS?" I asked.

"Yes," Mom said. "Scared of AIDS. That's scary enough for anybody. And scared of how people would respond when they found out. Scared that they would hate her, that they wouldn't have anything to do with her. That's scary, too, you know."

"Yeah, I guess so," I mumbled. "What's going to happen?" I asked Dad.

"A lot of parents want Natalie out of Woodburn. I don't agree, but I understand how they feel. Mr. Mohammadi has decided to call a community meeting this Thursday night to give everyone a chance to be heard. He'll make a decision after that. I just hope it's the right one."

"Whatever decision he does make," Mom added, "it won't be an easy one."

It was quiet for a few minutes.

"Is Natalie going to die?" I was trying my best to hold back my tears.

My Mom sighed a big sigh. "Probably so, dear."

"But can't somebody do something? Isn't there medicine they can give her?" It was no use: I couldn't hold my tears back any longer.

"There are treatments to help people with AIDS, Amy," Dad explained, "but there's no cure. I'm sorry."

"Sorry? Everybody's sorry." Now I was crying *and* shouting. "But nobody's doing anything. Nobody's helping Natalie. And I don't understand why."

"There are people who are working on this problem," Dad started to say, but I was too upset to hear about it.

"Will they be able to help Natalie?" was all I wanted to know.

Again the room grew silent. I had my answer.

CHAPTER 7

I knew I had to see Natalie. I wanted to tell her what everybody at Woodburn was talking about, and I wanted to hear what she had to say.

Natalie worked near the Woodburn School. It was an easy walk. I told my parents that I had to go to the library after school for a special project (another lie!) and walked the four blocks to Natalie's office.

"Amy Wilson! This is a surprise," Natalie said. "A very nice surprise." I had never seen Natalie at work before. She looked so nice and so happy. You could tell she really liked her job. "What brings you here?" she asked.

"Well, I missed the school bus, and I need a ride home," I answered. Listening to myself, I couldn't believe this was me talking, the Amy Wilson I had known for eleven years. I wasn't used to telling lies, and I didn't like it: it felt so sneaky. But I was doing it now, and getting pretty good at it, too.

"Do you mind if I make a quick stop first?" Natalie asked as we drove home. "I just want to tell Raymond why I'm leaving work early." Raymond was Natalie's husband. He was a lot of fun. He cooked hot dogs and hamburgers on the grill for the Video Club picnic. He wore a tall white hat and an apron that said, "Cookin' Ray's Way." And Ray's way was good! Those were the best hot dogs and hamburgers I ever had.

Ray was in the yard when we pulled into their driveway. "Bringing work home with you, dear?" he said, laughing. I think he meant me.

"Ray," Natalie said, "you remember Amy Wilson. From the Woodburn Video Club."

"Sure do," he said and stuck out his hand. "How are you, Amy?"

I could feel my old shyness creeping over me. "Fine," I tried to say, shaking his hand.

"Well, come on in for some fresh lemonade," he said, inviting us into the house, his arms around our shoulders. "I just took it out of the can."

"My husband," Natalie laughed, "Mr. Good Housekeeping."

I took a seat in the kitchen while Ray poured the lemonade. Natalie took a dish of fudge brownies out of the fridge and bit into one for a taste. "Hey, no free samples!" Ray shouted, playfully slapping her hand.

"Here," Natalie said, as she shoved the brownie in Ray's mouth. "Maybe you should taste it, too," she laughed.

"Not bad," Ray said approvingly. "Try it yourself."

Natalie licked her finger and smiled. "Not too bad. Not too bad for Mr. Good Housekeeping."

We sat at the kitchen table and drank the lemonade. Ray and Natalie chatted about different things—you know, everyday kinds of things, like the household chores and that sort of stuff. It reminded me of home.

"Hey," Natalie said, looking at me, "time to get you home." Sitting there, watching and listening to Ray and Natalie, I almost forgot about AIDS and the trouble at Woodburn. It was easy to do. Everything seemed so . . . well, so normal.

"Nice seeing you again, Amy," said Ray. Natalie kissed Ray goodbye, and we headed to the car. And I still hadn't asked her about AIDS. Where was my nerve? But I wasn't the only one who had something to talk about. I guess I wasn't the only one who needed to talk.

"I'm glad you missed your bus, Amy," Natalie said. I didn't look at her. "There's something I've been wanting to talk with you about." I don't know why, but I was so nervous all of a sudden I was shaking. It felt like there was a big lump in my throat. "Something important." Rather than go right home, Natalie stopped at Woodburn Park. I could see the lake out of the car window. There was a gentle breeze blowing the clouds around, and the surface of the lake was bright with changing colors and shapes.

"Amy," Natalie continued, "I'm afraid the days ahead are not going to be easy ones. Not for me and not for the children at

Woodburn. You're going to hear a lot of different things—a lot of wrong things—and I wanted to talk with you before rumors started"—

"It's too late," I shouted. "Everybody knows you have AIDS!" The "AIDS" word must have jarred loose the lump in my throat. I started to cry. I was crying and trying to talk at the same time, and all I could get out were words—"parents," "club," "meeting"—but Natalie got the idea. I could only get out one more word: "Why?"

Natalie was upset, too. "Let me try to explain."

"But it's too late," I interrupted. "It's too late to explain now! Everything is ruined." I went to see Natalie because I wanted an explanation, but now I couldn't listen. "I can get home by myself from here," I said as I got out of the car and started to walk away.

"Amy, please try to understand." Natalie got out on her side to walk after me. "I wanted to explain, but in the right place and at the right time. It just isn't that easy to sit down with someone and say, 'Guess what, I have AIDS.' Please, believe me."

"I believe you," I said. I remembered the crowd in the movie, the one with the burning torches, and how the light showed so many faces full of fear and hatred. "I really do."

We were both quiet for a while.

"I don't want you to hate me, Amy," Natalie said in almost a whisper.

I whispered back: "I don't."

"Let me take you home," she suggested.

"I'd rather walk," I said. "It's okay. I really can walk from here."

"Will you be all right?" Natalie asked.

Suddenly, I felt so selfish. Here was Natalie asking me if I would be all right. Who was asking Natalie if *she'd* be all right, if *she* felt lonely? Who was worrying about her?

"Sure," I said, "I'll be all right. I'd like to walk home alone."

I walked slowly for a minute or two, wondering what would happen to Natalie. When I looked back, I saw her standing beside the lake, staring straight ahead. I had a horrible feeling—just for a second, like a wave that washed over me—that I might never see Natalie again.

CHAPTER 8

The AIDS spell had cast its strangeness on Woodburn, too. The word about Natalie was now all over the school, and everywhere you looked, little groups were huddling together, talking in whispers and secretly glancing around.

I saw Robbie Jenkins, and before I could say hello, he handed me a note. "Don't say a word" was all he said, and in an instant he was gone.

"Now what is Robbie up to?" I wondered. I opened the note. It read: *Emergency Meeting! Woodburn Video Club. After School. All Club Members Must Attend! R.J.* "Robbie Jenkins," I said to myself, "whatever you're up to, I'll bet it's no good."

I somehow managed to get through the day without talking to anyone about Natalie. It seemed funny. I knew that's what everyone was whispering about, but there seemed to be an invisible wall around me, keeping the whispers away from me. I was at Woodburn, doing all the things I always do, but it was like I wasn't *really* there. It's hard to describe.

When the last bell rang, I hurried to the emergency meeting of the Video Club. This was Robbie's show from the very start. "It's time," he began the meeting, "to pick a new club sponsor. It's not too late: we can still enter our horror film in the video contest."

"And what about Natalie?" Jason asked.

"Natalie's out," Robbie said strongly. "There's going to be a meeting tonight, and she'll be kicked out of Woodburn—for good! Nobody is going to get near her again."

But Jason didn't give up—or give in. "Well, we can give her a chance tonight, can't we?"

"You can," Robbie shot back. "But not me or all the other kids who feel the same way I do. You have to choose sides. Are you going to be part of the new Woodburn Video Club or not?"

"I *would* like to make the movie," Brenda said.

"It's not our fault Natalie has AIDS," Leslie added. "If she can't sponsor the Video Club, then someone else will just have to. Isn't that right, Amy?" Leslie looked at me to answer, but I didn't say a word. I was too busy watching my friends turn into strangers.

"That's right," Robbie said. "And that's why I called this meeting. I want a vote to kick Natalie out as the Video Club sponsor. And I want to vote now. All those in favor"—

"No!" I said, and said it like I meant it. The AIDS spell had changed so many things, I guess it changed Amy Wilson, too. There wasn't any room for "Quiet Little Amy" anymore. I just had to say goodbye to her—once and for all. "No. We have to give Natalie a chance, a chance to explain. We have to find out

28

what AIDS is really about, what it really means. Natalie isn't some sort of monster: she's our friend. It's time we remembered that. It's time we started listening to her. And getting others to listen to her."

"And how are we supposed to do that?" asked Robbie.

"I don't know," I said after a moment. "I don't know."

"Well, I have an idea." And there stood Natalie.

CHAPTER 9

The AIDS information meeting was held in the Woodburn School auditorium. By the time I got there with my Mom and Dad, the place was packed. I mean, wall-to-wall people. It seemed like everyone I knew was there. Natalie was sitting in the first row. The air was filled with an angry buzzing sound. The room was already hot.

Mr. Mohammadi tried to bring the meeting to order. He was seated on the stage with several other people I didn't know. "Attention, everyone," he shouted above the noise of the crowd. I felt sorry for him. Mr. Mohammadi was only the assistant principal, but he had to be the real principal until a replacement was found for Mr. Yoder. I bet he wished they had found one by now. He sounded really nervous, and I knew how that felt.

"Attention, please," he said again, as the crowd began to quiet. "All of us are here tonight because we care about our children, because we care about what's best for them. I hope we can keep the welfare of our children foremost in our minds tonight as we talk about a very difficult subject, a subject surrounded by ignorance and the fear bred of ignorance. We're here tonight because we are concerned. Let's keep that"—

"Let's keep Natalie Gregg away from our children," a man shouted from the audience. It sounded like Robbie's father. There were shouts of "Yeah!" from some and "Quiet!" from others. I took hold of my Mom's hand.

Mr. Mohammadi tried to restore order. "We will get to the question of Natalie Gregg. Before we open the meeting to discussion, however, I think it would be a good idea to learn a little bit more about AIDS. There may be some things that surprise you"—

"We don't need any more surprises!" someone in the audience hollered.

Mr. Mohammadi continued. "Let me introduce Dr. David Reed, the director of Public Health Services at the Woodburn Community Medical Center. Some of you may already know him. I hope all of you will listen to what Dr. Reed has to say."

Dr. Reed advanced to the podium. He didn't look nervous at all. You got the feeling that this was not the first AIDS information meeting he had been to, that he had talked to angry parents before. But it was sure hard to believe he had ever faced a crowd like this one.

"Good evening," he began. "To start our discussion tonight, I brought with me a brief video on the subject of AIDS. Perhaps it will help you better understand this disease. Will someone turn off the lights, please?"

Mr. Mohammadi switched off the lights. The hall went dark, except for the small spot of light from the video screen on stage. The video showed another doctor talking to a group of people about AIDS. I couldn't understand what he was saying. He was talking about things called antigens and retroviruses. He was talking about bodily fluids and immunity. But the only thing I knew was that he was talking way over my head. And I wasn't the only one, either. I could see that most people weren't paying attention. I guess it was over their heads as well.

"What does this have to do with Natalie?" I asked. My Mom just squeezed my hand in response.

When the lights came back on, the angry buzzing sound came back, too. Before Dr. Reed could speak again, questions were being shouted at him.

One voice spoke louder than the others: "Is my son going to get AIDS now?"

"No," he said. "AIDS is not spread by casual contact"—

"How do you know for sure?" someone interrupted.

"We can't take any chances!" came another voice.

"Would you take a chance with *your* child?" came another.

And another: "She doesn't belong in the school!"

And another: "They had snacks together!"

"She doesn't belong! She doesn't belong!"

The buzzing sound grew until it seemed to roar from the angry crowd. Mr. Mohammadi again spoke to restore order. "Please," he pleaded, "let's give Dr. Reed a chance." Some parents agreed. There were shouts of "Let's hear him," but not enough of them: most of the people just wouldn't listen.

And that's when I stood up, took the deepest breath of my life, grabbed my backpack, and walked toward the stage. It was the hardest thing I had ever done.

"Amy? Amy, where are you going?" Mom asked nervously. "Come back here."

But I was gone, heading for the steps that led to the stage. "Well," I said mostly to myself, "this is it." I was so scared I could barely grip the strap on my backpack. When I climbed up to the stage, my knees felt like they were made out of jelly.

The audience grew quieter as I made my way to the podium. Mr. Mohammadi looked at me with a mixture of wonder and fright. He was speechless. "Please, Mr. Mohammadi," I said, "I have something to say."

"But . . . but . . . but" was all he could get out. He sounded like a little motorboat going around in circles. Dr. Reed moved a chair to the podium for me to stand on.

"Excuse me," I began, sounding like a squeaky gerbil trying to get someone's attention. ("Come on," I thought, "you said goodbye to the old Amy. It's time to meet the new one.") "Excuse me," I said again. "My name is Amy Wilson. I go to the Woodburn School and Community Center. I am in the fifth grade." The crowd was quiet now. One woman even smiled at me. I tried to keep my eyes on her. "I am also a member of the Video Club. Natalie Gregg is my friend."

"That's Mike Wilson's little girl," I heard someone say. "What's she doing up there?"

"This afternoon we had an emergency meeting of the Video Club. Natalie was there, too. We talked about AIDS. And we taped it all on our video equipment. We call this tape *Friends for Life*. I'd like you to see it now." I reached into my backpack and handed a video cassette to Mr. Mohammadi. He looked sick. "Please," I said.

"Let's turn off the lights," he said in return.

Once again, the room went dark. When the video started, you could see everyone sitting in a circle. Robbie said that he didn't want to be in the movie, but he would hold the video camera. ("Well, *someone* has to direct you guys," he said.) When everyone was seated, Robbie began to film. "Okay. *Friends for Life*. Take your places. And, *ACTION!*"

CHAPTER 10

Natalie was the first to speak. She took a deep breath and broke the silence.

"First of all," she started, "I owe you all an apology. You're my friends, and I wish I had told you I had AIDS as soon as I found out. I wish I had told your parents and teachers, too. I'm sorry. But it's just so hard to tell people. You know, there's so much fear out there, and so much anger, and so much . . . hatred. I didn't want you to be afraid of me, and I didn't want you to be angry with me. I don't want you to hate me. But I guess you have a right to be mad."

"We sure do," mumbled Robbie.

"I don't blame you a bit," continued Natalie. "But now I'm here, and you can ask me anything you like. I may not be able to explain it all to you. There are some things I don't understand. There are some things that only your teachers or parents can tell you. But I'll do the best I can."

"Are you . . . going to die?" Leslie asked. I could tell she was upset.

There was a tiny smile on Natalie's face when she spoke. "Well, Leslie, that's certainly a direct question." She paused for a moment and took another deep breath. "We're all going to die sooner or later, Leslie. I hope in your case it's a long, long time away. But in my case, it's probably not. Yes, it's likely that I'm going to die. AIDS, in most cases, is a terminal disease. That means if you get it, you're going to die. Some people live with it longer than others, but there is no cure."

34

"Aren't you afraid to die?" Jason asked.

"Yes, I guess I am. But I'm more sad than afraid. Sad to lose my friends. Sad to lose Ray. But, still, I'm glad I know about it now, so I can plan for the time ahead, so I can make the most of whatever time I have. Making the most of our time: that's something we all have to do."

"But how did *you* get it?" asked Brenda. "I mean, you know, . . . AIDS."

"You won't get it by saying the word, Brenda," Natalie responded. "But that's a good question. Some people have pretty wild ideas about how you get AIDS. They think you can get it just by being near someone who has it. Or by drinking from the same glass someone with AIDS has used. Or by using the same toilet seat. Or swimming in the same pool. Some people even think you can get it from a mosquito bite. But none of these things are true.

"It's not easy to get AIDS. You can't just catch AIDS like a cold or the flu, and you don't have to worry that you will. It's just not spread that way. You won't get it through everyday contact with the people around you. Not at school, or work, or home."

"Then how *did* you get it?" Brenda asked again.

"Well, I don't know everything about AIDS, but I'll try to explain. AIDS is caused by a virus, like many other diseases. The AIDS virus lives in the human body, and it can live there for years without seeming to cause any problems. But it attacks

and breaks down your body's ability to fight diseases. That's called the body's immune system—all the things your body can do to keep you from getting sick.

"People with AIDS can't fight off sicknesses the way healthy people can. They have what is called an 'immune deficiency.' In other words, the AIDS virus weakens the body's immune system. That's why the virus is called the Human Immunodeficiency Virus—or HIV, for short. In most cases, a person with the HIV virus, sooner or later, will see the signs—what doctors call the symptoms or the syndrome—of this problem in their own immune system."

"Wow," I said. "This is pretty complicated."

"I guess so, and I'm no expert either," said Natalie. "But think about the word *AIDS*. That's A-I-D-S. It means Acquired Immune Deficiency Syndrome. People with AIDS have acquired a deficiency in their immune system. The long and short of it is that the AIDS virus means they are going to get very sick. It means they are probably going to die."

"But I still don't understand," Brenda said again, "how the AIDS virus gets from one person to another."

"AIDS is spread," Natalie explained, "in two main ways. You can get AIDS if you share a drug needle with someone who has the AIDS virus."

"But you don't use drugs!" I said excitedly. "You don't, do you, Natalie?"

"No, I don't," she said. "And AIDS is just one reason why you shouldn't either. One way not to get AIDS is to never, *never* use drugs."

"I'm *never* getting a shot from the doctor again," Leslie claimed. "That's for sure."

"No, no," I interrupted. "The doctor will only use clean needles. Right, Natalie?"

"That's right," she said. "There is absolutely no harm in getting a shot from the doctor. But you must never use a needle that's been used before. Don't even play with one."

"What's the other way you can get AIDS?" Jason asked.

"This is a very sensitive subject. It's something you should talk about with your parents. The other way you can get AIDS is by having sex with someone who has the virus."

We were all quiet for a while, too embarrassed to speak. For a moment I thought we would have to stop the video. That is, until Robbie broke the silence. "You mean, 'doing it'?" he asked.

Leslie, Brenda, and I started to giggle. But we could tell that Natalie didn't think it was funny. She looked right at Robbie and spoke softly to him.

"Sex, Robbie, is one way people who are in love show their love for one another. It is a very special expression of love and something that you will learn much more about as you grow older. What I want you to know now is that when you are ready to have sex, it is something you must think about carefully, it is something you must do safely, and it is something you must do with love and honesty."

"I know what sex is," Jason said. "It's when you have babies. It's like when a man and a woman get together to have babies. I know all about it."

"Well, there's a little more to sex than that, Jason," Natalie said; "but having babies is part of it."

"But I thought only queers got AIDS," Robbie said. "You know, fairies."

"I want everyone to listen to me carefully." Natalie said. "I don't want to hear words like 'fairies' or 'queers' or 'fags.' They are simply not the right words to use. If we want to talk about this, we'll treat all people with respect and talk about them in the same way. Robbie is talking about people who are 'homosexual' or 'gay.' That is what they want to be called, and that is what we will call them. Is that understood?"

We all nodded that we agreed. Even Robbie. "Okay," he said, "Let me start again. I thought only gay guys got AIDS."

"Wrong," Natalie said firmly. "That's very wrong. Everyone—men and women, whether they are gay or not—can get AIDS. And that's why it's so important to talk about it. You can't try to hide from it. You have to know about it, to know the truth about it—to know how you can get it and how *not* to get it. You can get AIDS by having sex with someone who has the AIDS virus, and that's why you must be responsible."

"Like what?" Leslie asked.

"Like waiting until you're old enough: till you're old enough to know what sex is all about—how important it is, how important it is to find someone you truly love, someone you want to be with for the rest of your life—that is part of the answer. Not all of it, but an important part of the answer."

"I read in a magazine," Leslie said, "that you should use a condom when you . . . you know, 'do it'? Can you please explain that to me?"

40

"I wish I could answer all of your questions," Natalie replied, "but it would be better if you talked to your parents about these things. This is a very important subject for parents to discuss with their children."

"But I tried to talk about it with them," Brenda said, "and they just told me to wait. They kept saying, 'When you're older, when you're older . . .'"

"Well, I talked about it with my parents!" I said. "We read this report together." I held up my copy of the "Message from the Surgeon General." It was pretty worn by now because my Mom and Dad and I had spent a lot of time reading it. "And it says right here"—

"Hold on a minute, Amy," Natalie said suddenly. "I want to try to explain something. As I said, it's very important for children to know about AIDS. It's very important for parents to help their children understand the issues. But it has to be up to the parents to decide the best time and the best way to do this.

"I know that you hear about sex all the time. You see it on television, and you can hear about it in the music you listen to. And I know it's confusing to you. Of course, you want to know more about it. I also know that some of your parents won't want to talk about it. But I think if you explain to them why you're concerned, your parents *will* understand—and they *will* want to help.

"In fact, *they* may need more information about AIDS. Ask them about the Surgeon General's report: if they've read it, if you can read it together. Let them know that there are places they can call for more information, like the Centers for Disease Control or the U.S. Public Health Service AIDS Hotline. Your teachers and counselors, your local school board, your family doctor—they will all be glad to help.

"Talking about sex is a special moment for parents and their children. Because of AIDS, families must talk about sex openly and honestly. We just can't put our heads in the sand. You need to learn about it. It may not be easy, but don't give up."

"But I still don't understand," Brenda exclaimed, "how *you* got AIDS."

"I got AIDS from having sex with my husband Raymond. He had the AIDS virus, although we didn't know it."

"How did you find out you had it?" I asked.

"It seemed like I was sick all the time. Finally, I went to the doctor, and he ordered a blood test. The test showed that I had the AIDS virus."

"But if Raymond gave it to you," I said, "why wasn't he sick?"

"Some people have the virus in their body," Natalie said, "but they don't show any signs of it. They don't feel or look sick. But they can pass it on to others. The only way to tell for sure if you're 'carrying' the AIDS virus is to have a blood test."

"Well, how did Raymond get it?" I asked.

Natalie sighed even more deeply before she answered. "Raymond got AIDS by sharing a needle. A needle that someone else had already used."

"Why?"

"He was using the needle because he was on drugs," she said. "It was a very bad time in Ray's life. I don't really want to talk about it too much. I think it should be Ray who talks about it—if he wants to. But one thing I know he would tell you: no matter how bad things look at the moment, turning to drugs is not the answer. It can only make matters worse. It can only hurt you. It could even kill you."

"Users are losers," Robbie said.

"That's right," added Natalie. "Ray got himself off drugs with the help of a lot of good people, and I'm very proud of him. But he got the AIDS virus from using a needle someone else had used, and he passed the virus on to me."

"But didn't you just want to kill him?" shouted Brenda. "Didn't you want to divorce him, at least?"

"Yes. I really did," Natalie said. "I just couldn't believe this had happened to me. Of course, I was mad. I was so mad I almost left Ray for good. But I love him, and I know that he loves me. We're going to see this thing through together." Natalie's voice lowered a little bit. "One of the worst things about AIDS is that it's such a . . . lonely disease. People don't want to be near you—even your friends, *even* your family. I want to have Ray there. I want to have my friends and my family there. I don't want to die alone."

"Will Ray get AIDS?" I asked. I didn't realize I had so many questions about AIDS inside me.

"Most likely, he will," answered Natalie. "Doctors think that people who have the virus will probably get AIDS, though it may take some time for the signs or symptoms to appear."

"There's no cure?" Jason asked.

"No cure," said Natalie. "It may take years to find one. The best thing to do is to be a responsible person. Don't do drugs. Don't have sex until you're grown up. Learn the facts. Talk to your parents. If you do that, there's nothing to be afraid of. Remember: you can't get AIDS from everyday contact with a person who has it. If you know someone who has AIDS, help them. Try to understand how *they* feel. They need your friendship and support—*they need your love*—now more than ever."

CHAPTER 11

That was the end of our video. I asked for the lights to be turned back on. I stood at the podium again.

"Thank you for watching our tape," I said. "I know that you came here because you're concerned about us, because you love us. But we want you to know that we care about Natalie, too. She's not just *our* friend: she's *your* friend, too. And, also"—I couldn't think of what else to say. I reached again into my backpack. This time I took out a new tee shirt. "We made this for Natalie," I said, as I held it up for everyone to see. "It says 'Friends for Life.' It's the official Woodburn School Video Club tee shirt. And I want the very first one to go to our club sponsor, Natalie Gregg."

"This is outrageous," I heard someone say. I saw several families leaving the meeting in a hurry. Robbie's parents looked very upset. Brenda's, too.

I took the tee shirt over to Natalie. She gave me a big hug. I heard people clapping and watched as little meetings started up all over the auditorium. I couldn't believe how many people liked the video. "You've got quite a little girl there, Mike," I heard someone say to my father. "Little?" I said to myself. I didn't feel little. And I didn't feel quiet anymore, either.

When we got home that night, it was after midnight, but I still couldn't sleep. I realized that I had left something back at the meeting. I left "Quiet Little Amy" back there.

I didn't know exactly who the new Amy was going to be, but I had a hunch I was going to like her. I had a hunch I was going to like her a lot!

CHAPTER 12

Several weeks passed before a decision was made about Natalie. She was finally allowed to remain as the Video Club sponsor. You had to have your parents' permission to join the club. Most of the original members stayed on (Robbie had to drop out), and a few new members joined. But soon after the AIDS meeting, Natalie got too sick to continue. We had a nice goodbye party.

We entered *Friends for Life* in the video contest and won an "Honorable Mention." It was an exciting time for all of us. Even Robbie came to the awards dinner. But Natalie was not well enough to attend.

I saw her several months after that. We met at the lake in Woodburn Park and sat on a nearby bench. She looked pale and thin. I could see she had been sick for a long time.

"Well, don't look like you've just seen a ghost," she joked. "I'm not one. Not yet, anyway."

We talked about her sickness. I asked her about Ray; she asked about the Video Club. She was sorry she had missed the awards dinner; she was glad Robbie was there. "I always liked Robbie," she said.

"Now isn't that awful," she went on, "talking in the past tense like that. That could get to be a bad habit." Natalie was trying, I'm sure, to make me feel better, but I think she could tell it wasn't working. "Look, Amy, I don't want to die. But the fact is that most people with AIDS will die. There's nothing I can do to change that. What I *can* do—with each day I have left—is to try to change the way people think about AIDS, to make people see that there is a human face and there are human feelings behind this disease. If I can do that"—

She stopped suddenly. "Let me read you something," she said. "It's a quotation I especially like. It's by a man named Robert Kennedy. He died young, too. I keep it with me all the time now." And she read it to me:

> *Each time a man stands up for an ideal or acts to improve the lot of others or strikes out against injustice, he sends forth a tiny ripple of hope, and crossing each other from a million different centers of energy and daring, those ripples build a current that can sweep down the mightiest walls of oppression and resistance.*

"And that goes for women, too," I said.

I didn't understand the quotation Natalie read, at least not all of it. But I knew it was about standing up for what you believe, no matter what other people do or say. I knew it was about not being afraid—and the difference that not being afraid can make.

"Yes, it goes for women, too," Natalie agreed with a smile. "I really believe," she said, "that we did send out one tiny ripple of hope to join the others. Together, we did that. And because we did that, my death will mean something—to others and to myself.

"And I'm especially proud of you because you stood up: you stood up to make other people think. And I know that you will keep on standing up for what you believe."

We sat longer, but after a while Natalie said she was getting tired and should be heading home. Just before she said goodbye, she gave me the slip of paper with her favorite quotation on it. "Here," she said, "you keep this." When I said I couldn't take it, she said, "Yes, I want you to keep it. It's for . . . well, it's for you, Amy."

I held the paper tightly in my hand as Natalie walked to her car.

I sat by the lake for a long time that day. Watching the ripples.

About The Kids on the Block

Founded in 1977 by Barbara Aiello, The Kids on the Block puppet program was formed to introduce young audiences to the topic of children with disabilities. Since then the goals and programs of The Kids on the Block have evolved and broadened to encompass a wide spectrum of individual differences and social concerns.

Barbara Aiello is nationally recognized for her work in special education. The former editor of *Teaching Exceptional Children*, Ms. Aiello has won numerous awards for her work with The Kids on the Block, including the President's Committee on Employment of the Handicapped Distinguished Service Award, the Easter Seal Communications Award for Outstanding Public Service, and the Epilepsy Foundation of America's Outstanding Achievement Award. Her puppets have appeared in all 50 states and throughout the world. In addition, over 1,000 groups in the United States and abroad make The Kids on the Block puppets an effective part of their community programs.

For More Information

The Kids on the Block
9385-C Gerwig Lane
Columbia, Maryland 21046
800-368-KIDS

Centers for Disease Control
Center for Health Promotion
and Education
Division of Health Education
1600 Clifton Rd.
Building 3   Room B16 (A14)
Atlanta, GA 30333
404-639-3824

AIDS Action Council
2033 M St., NW
Suite 801
Washington, DC 20036
202-293-2886

American Foundation for AIDS
Research
Executive Office
5900 Wilshire Blvd.
Second Floor, East Satellite
Los Angeles, CA 90036
213-857-5900

National AIDS Network
2033 M St., NW
Suite 800
Washington, DC 20036
202-293-2437

Hotlines

Centers for Disease Control
800-342-AIDS

U.S. Public Health Service
800-447-AIDS